# Dear Parent:

Congratulations! Your child is taking the first steps on an exciting journey. The destination? Independent reading!

**STEP INTO READING®** will help your child get there. The program offers five steps to reading success. Each step includes fun stories and colorful art. There are also Step into Reading Sticker Books, Step into Reading Math Readers, Step into Reading Write-In Readers, Step into Reading Phonics Readers, and Step into Reading Phonics First Steps! Boxed Sets—a complete literacy program with something for every child.

## Learning to Read, Step by Step!

**Ready to Read   Preschool–Kindergarten**
• big type and easy words • rhyme and rhythm • picture clues
For children who know the alphabet and are eager to begin reading.

**Reading with Help   Preschool–Grade 1**
• basic vocabulary • short sentences • simple stories
For children who recognize familiar words and sound out new words with help.

**Reading on Your Own   Grades 1–3**
• engaging characters • easy-to-follow plots • popular topics
For children who are ready to read on their own.

**Reading Paragraphs   Grades 2–3**
• challenging vocabulary • short paragraphs • exciting stories
For newly independent readers who read simple sentences with confidence.

**Ready for Chapters   Grades 2–4**
• chapters • longer paragraphs • full-color art
For children who want to take the plunge into chapter books but still like colorful pictures.

**STEP INTO READING®** is designed to give every child a successful reading experience. The grade levels are only guides. Children can progress through the steps at their own speed, developing confidence in their reading, no matter what their grade.

Remember, a lifetime love of reading starts with a single step!

*For my sweet Lilly*
*—M.L.*

Visit us on the Web!
www.stepintoreading.com
www.randomhouse.com/kids

Educators and librarians, for a variety of teaching tools, visit us at
www.randomhouse.com/teachers

*Library of Congress Cataloging-in-Publication Data*
Lagonegro, Melissa.
    The perfect dress / by Melissa Lagonegro ; illustrated by Elisa Marrucchi. — 1st ed.
        p. cm. — (Step into reading. Step 2 book)
    ISBN 978-0-7364-2558-2 (trade) — ISBN 978-0-7364-8063-5 (lib. bdg.)
    I. Marrucchi, Elisa, ill. II. Title.
    PZ8.3.L1363Pe 2009
    [E]—dc22
    2008003478

Printed in the United States of America    16 15                    First Edition

## The Perfect Dress

By Melissa Lagonegro

Illustrated by Elisa Marrucchi

Random House 🏠 New York

Dust and dirt
make a mess!

Cinderella needs
a brand-new dress.

Clean and bright.
Oh, what fun!

This blue dress is
the perfect one.

Jasmine must choose

a skirt or a gown.

Her friend Rajah
looks on with a frown.

Jasmine and Aladdin
enjoy a starry night!

Her green outfit
is truly just right.

Belle is excited about the fancy feast!

She gets dressed for
her date with the Beast.

Belle and the Beast

share a night of romance.

Her yellow gown is
perfect for this dance.

Everyone sings in
the wedding parade!

King Triton sends off
his little mermaid!

Ariel's wedding dress
fits just right.

# Prince Eric thinks she looks lovely in white!

Sleeping Beauty has
such a busy day!

The fairies can help.

They are on their way!

Music and menus.

There is much to do.

Should Aurora's dress
be pink or dark blue?

The Prince arrives with
his horse by his side.

Snow White must dress
for their royal ride.

It's chilly and windy.

It feels like a storm.

A blue and red cape will keep Snow White warm.

Slip on the shoes.

# Fluff up the dress.

Put on the jewelry.

# Look your best.

Which one do you think

is the perfect dress?